All for Naught

—

The Rise and Fall of
President Barry Blue

Books by M.E. Sharpe

Non-Fiction

JOHN KENNETH GALBRAITH AND THE LOWER ECONOMICS

AMERICA IN DECLINE

CHANCE ENCOUNTERS
A Memoir (Forthcoming)

Fiction and Poetry

THOU SHALT NOT KILL UNLESS OTHERWISE INSTRUCTED

REQUIEM FOR NEW ORLEANS

CANDIDE THE TENTH AND OTHER AGITATIONS

YOU NEVER CAN TELL
and SMOG
Two Novellas

ALL FOR NAUGHT *and*
THE RISE AND FALL OF
PRESIDENT BARRY BLUE
Two Novellas

All for Naught

Two Novellas

The Rise and Fall of President Barry Blue

M.E. Sharpe

Routledge
Taylor & Francis Group

LONDON AND NEW YORK

First published 2014 by M.E. Sharpe

Published 2015 by Routledge
2 Park Square, Milton Park, Abingdon, Oxon OX14 4RN
711 Third Avenue, New York, NY 10017, USA

Routledge is an imprint of the Taylor & Francis Group, an informa business

Sharpe, M. E.
  [Novellas. Selections]
  All for naught ; The rise and fall of President Barry Blue : Two novellas / by M.E. Sharpe.
     pages cm
  ISBN 978-0-7656-4541-8 (pbk. : alk. paper)
  I. Sharpe, M. E., Rise and fall of President Barry Blue. II. Title.

PS3619.H356648A79 2014
813'.6—dc23   2013046117

ISBN 13: 9780765645418 (pbk)

To my wife Carole; my children Susanna, Matthew, Elisabeth, and Hana; my sons-in-law Sergio and Alex; and my daughter-in-law Mystelle

Contents

Acknowledgments

For the impeccable work of Angela Piliouras, production manager; Susanna Sharpe, copy editor; Nancy Connick, typesetter; Liz Dancho, author photographer; Jesse Sanchez, cover and interior designer; and Carole Brafman Sharpe, advisor-in-chief.

All for Naught

Contents

Chapter One

An Explosion

A terrific explosion demolished the foyer about five in the morning. The estate manager called the police. The police checked the grounds and came up with one critical piece of evidence. A five-foot stone wall surrounded the fifteen-acre grounds. A grainy picture from the surveillance camera showed someone climbing over the rear wall from a wooded area. He or she—it's not clear if it was a man or was a woman wearing loose clothing—he or she carried some kind of package, explosives no doubt. The explosion knocked out the surveillance system so no further pictures were available.

John Stevens, the estate manager, spoke to the police chief and asked him to keep the report of the incident confidential. He also instructed the household staff to do the same. He didn't want any copycats to try again. He assumed that the intent of the mysterious figure was assassination, assassination of the estate owner, Richard Melmont, who had enemies. He didn't want to give out that any would-be murderer could just climb over the stone wall and blow up the house, or at least part of it. Stevens would explain to neighbors and the local press that a gas line had exploded, and that would be the end of it. There was no gas line leading to the foyer, but no matter.

Richard Melmont lived alone in a Greek Revival mansion located in back-country Greenwich. He and his wife Maria had amiably agreed to live in separate houses, but conduct the public side of their lives together. Their children Barbara and Daniel were grown and visited occasionally.

By eight in the morning, Stevens had called a trusted contractor and explained the need to reconstruct the foyer in five days, by Saturday. Mr. Melmont had planned a luncheon and among his guests were an Under Secretary of Defense, the ambassador from France, and the ambassador from Great Britain. You may think that five days is not enough time to reconstruct a foyer. But when a sufficient amount of money flows, men can perform miracles. And miracles were performed. Meanwhile, the estate manager arranged to have furniture, carpets, paintings, and a grand chandelier appear at precisely the right moment. A sufficient amount of money flowed and by late Friday afternoon, the foyer and its contents were as good as new—because they were new.

Chapter Two

Maria Melmont Lunches with Her Children

Maria Melmont sat staring at a blank screen on her computer. She lived not a mile away from Richard Melmont in a more modest mansion. She began thinking about possibilities. The intruder was a foreign terrorist who wanted to make a statement by killing one of the richest men in the United States, in his view an evil man. The intruder was an American terrorist who wanted to make a statement by killing a member of the one percent, indeed of the one-hundredth of one percent. The intruder had a personal grudge against Mr. Melmont. Her thoughts began to suggest a story line. Maria Melmont was a novelist with several successful titles to her credit. But at the moment she was not interested in a story line. She was interested in finding out who tried to kill her husband. Or warn him. After all, who is in the foyer at five in the morning?

Her children Barbara and Daniel were coming for lunch. They are hardly children. But that designation seems to apply to offspring of any age. Barbara is a lawyer who graduated from Harvard Law School five years ago and has had experience working for a prestigious firm. Daniel is an economist who graduated from Harvard University three years ago and teaches Keynesian theory at The New School University. I need hardly add that they are legacies, since Richard Melmont received his MBA from Harvard Business School and since has opened his pocket wide for that institution.

"We must go to your father and tell him to get out of the limelight." Maria Melmont was accustomed to speaking categorically.

"What if he gets out of the limelight? He's a billionaire. Billionaires are in the limelight whether they like it or not." Barbara Melmont was accustomed to speaking reasonably.

"Let him give his billions to worthy causes. Then he will be seen as a good billionaire." So replied mother.

"You know very well that we cannot tell father what to do," Barbara speaking, Daniel nodding in agreement. "I hear that he has something more ghastly afoot than anything he has done before."

Mother: "I have not heard of it. What could be more ghastly than telling all his trusting investors that the market was about to go up when he knew that the market was about to go down, fleecing them of several billion?"

Daniel: "You know his answer, mother. They should have looked at history, as father did."

Mother: "I shall go and ask him what is the point of making more billions on top of the billions he already has. Go and do something useful."

Barbara: "I should rather go to Africa and stamp out HIV than make billions. Billions make my life difficult. I never know if a man is interested in me or my future trust fund."

Daniel: "I have the same problem. Except in my case it is more of an opportunity than a problem. At least in the short run."

After lunch, Maria began ruminating about the novel and the danger to her husband, getting the two mixed up in her mind. In any case, I shall use my magic to provide a grand luncheon for Richard, the Under Secretary, the ambassadors, and other assorted notables who come Saturday. I wonder what more ghastly thing Richard has in mind than anything he has done before?

Chapter Three

The Device

Richard Melmont regularly invited ten or twelve accomplished people for lunch on Saturdays. Part of his motive was to keep up with what was going on. Part was to enlarge his group of acquaintances. Part was to enjoy genial conversation. Part was to make known the extent of his influence. And of course part was to call in a favor when needed.

The luncheons started with conversation in the foyer, now the new foyer, followed by a short tour of the public rooms, with comments by Melmont on his superb art collection and explanations of when and where photographs had been taken, in which he appeared with well-known celebrities. The lunch followed, during which he expounded on a current topic, followed by a leisurely discussion by his guests. Most left quite satisfied to have been included in such august company.

The menu was planned by Maria Melmont, who was invariably present. I shall buy the flowers, she thought, reflecting on the upcoming Saturday. Chicken Marsala with white rice and green beans would be just the thing, served with Veuve Clicquot and tiramisu for dessert.

Just that the forthcoming lunch meeting was not the usual lunch meeting. When the British and French ambassadors, the Under Secretary of Defense, several members of the Senate Armed Services Committee, and Richard Melmont meet for lunch, it is no ordinary lunch. Mrs. Melmont was quite on edge. Additional security was on hand. Additional security had, in fact, been on hand to monitor the premises since the day of the bombing.

The usual pleasantries were exchanged in the foyer. The usual tour of the paintings and photographs took place. Then the group proceeded to the dining room. A discussion ensued about economic and political stresses in various parts of the world, the difficulty in seeing an exit in the next decade or longer.

I control laboratories in the United States and France that have been working on a new weapons system. Melmont turned to his subject. They have converged on making a device that is capable of killing masses of people. Two things are unusual about it. It kills but does not destroy property. It uses a strong subatomic force and therefore is not a chemical weapon. I immediately realized that this device is not outlawed by the Chemical Weapons Convention. Moreover, it can be aimed at a specific area, a few miles in diameter or a few hundred miles in diameter. The device can be carried by a missile or a plane. We must be the first to develop it. We must keep it out of the hands of every hostile power. We must have the full support of the American, French, and British governments in developing this weapon. I have invested considerable funds for research and development. I am prepared to invest additional funds to manufacture the weapon on a sufficient scale to deter all other states from even thinking of it. If any war should take place with this weapon, we would have no need to invest in reconstruction. All the roads, bridges, buildings, and their contents would remain intact.

Everyone in the room was stunned. Maria Melmont's heart raced. The evil of it. The evil of it, she thought. The others thought likewise. But their thoughts raced ahead.

Richard Melmont voiced their thoughts. We have in our hands a terrifying device. If we are ever forced to use it, we are evil. If someone else uses it first, we are even more evil. We have no choice. We are forced to choose a lesser evil to avoid a greater one. Is this not always the case in war? And in much of life? Let us look at it this way. We have in our hands a device to prevent all war.

Chapter Four

Daniel Melmont Becomes a Banker

Daniel Melmont was hardly satisfied teaching economics at the New School. There was no future in it for him. He had not found a purpose in life except to rid the world of evil, and he could not rid the world of evil by teaching at the New School. He could not turn to his father, who took the world as he found it, evil or not. An opportunity arose to get started on something useful through a friend of his mother, a well-known epidemiologist who had made significant contributions to the ultimate eradication of HIV. Arthur Kutner had decided to give up his practice and devote himself full time to research. He found a small investment bank that would provide sufficient income to give him the freedom he needed. The president of BT Bank had in mind retiring in several years and wanted to sell out to an investor who would eventually succeed him as president, a position that would require little more than a periodic meeting with the rest of the board.

Kutner knew little about investment banking, but he quickly grasped the concept and saw that BT Bank was growing at a healthy rate. Kutner became partners with the founder and owner, Jack Bugler, who was aptly named, for he had both the voice and manner of someone sounding a forward march for his troops. By contrast, Kutner was soft-spoken and genial. The two men were opposites.

Through Maria Melmont's intermediation, Richard Melmont was induced to make a substantial investment in the firm with the understanding that Daniel would be given a job. From Daniel's point of view, what better way to begin eradicating evil from the world than by contributing to Dr. Kutner's work. He became secretary of the bank.

The investment proved to be disastrous. Kutner's investment, Melmont's investment, everyone's investment proved to be disastrous. The rosy glow of the financial statement was not a sign of health but of illness, severe illness. After a year bathing in the rosy glow, Dr. Kutner became suspicious. Where were the considerable profits coming from? The principal clients, four large department stores, were not doing well. A careful study of the books showed that the stores were being sustained by the infusion of ever larger sums of money. At some point the pyramid would crash. By then Mr. Bugler would have sold his assets in BT Bank and would have retired.

The board was in a state of consternation. Bugler was forced to resign. Two factions formed. In spite of the facts, half were old friends of Bugler and were still loyal to him. The other half were new investors loyal to Kutner. A fight ensued about who would succeed to the presidency. Someone came up with the brilliant idea of appointing the neophyte Daniel Melmont president, someone too innocent to belong to one faction or the other. He was duly approached. He said yes. President of a multi-million-dollar corporation at age twenty-six had a certain appeal.

Then Arthur Kutner had a heart attack. He had thought, put all your eggs in one basket then watch the basket. He had not watched carefully enough. After weeks in the hospital, he returned home in the care of his wife. But he was on the phone every day with Daniel. Daniel was on his side. Daniel even loved him. But he refused to talk about business on the assumption that Kutner would become even more stressed.

Either way, to talk or not to talk, stressed Kutner. He died over a stupid investment in a stupid business.

That terrible blow and the daily stress of managing a failing business and attempting to manage a board of wild horses pulling in opposite directions drained Daniel to the point of exhaustion. Every day he went home feeling despair. He had to quit. But at the critical moment the board decided that no one could withdraw his investment until the crisis was resolved. Not that it could be resolved. Daniel's dream of doing good by such roundabout means was shattered. He had one very potent move left to make. He would go to the regional office of the Federal Reserve Board and lay the entire sordid story before them. An exception was made for Daniel Melmont and he withdrew his investment, or rather his father's investment. He went to console Dr. Kutner's widow. But she wanted more consolation than Daniel was prepared to give.

Daniel Melmont in Love

Daniel Melmont was an heir to a great fortune. So it was assumed by those given to making such assumptions, particularly mothers of daughters who have little prospect of acquiring their own great fortune except by marrying it. One such mother, Isabelle Alenski, had just such a daughter, Ilana, a charming young woman of no particular distinction, who happened to have been a high school friend of Daniel Melmont. What could be more natural than for Isabelle Alenski to invite a group of Ilana's high school friends to a gala dinner at the Alenskis', especially including Daniel Melmont? It was understood between Isabelle Alenski and Ilana Alenski that she was to be particularly charming with Daniel and in fact sit next to him at the table. She was so charming that next day Daniel emailed Ilana asking for a date, much to the delight and satisfaction of mother Alenski.

The young woman was receptive to Daniel's radical ideas about redeeming the world, so much so that he was quite taken with her and wondered why he had not noticed her in high school. Yes, he had noticed her, but they had traveled in different circles. Not for the first time had someone wondered why he or she had not been more attracted to the other he or she earlier in life. After an evening out, she invited him back to her home, saying that he could have anything that he wanted, referring to drinks, but the remark could be easily misinterpreted. Some serious petting ensued, but Daniel was still a novice, and petting was the end of it. As a high school student, he had been invited home by several female teachers, ostensibly to discuss an assignment, and though he found the teachers attractive, he didn't know what to do about it and neither did the teachers. He periodically visited the widowed mother of a high school friend even when the friend was away at college, and she always kissed him full on the mouth as he was leaving, she saying something about the strength of her need. But nothing further came of it.

After several months, Daniel became passionate about Ilana and Ilana appeared equally passionate about Daniel. Mrs. Alinski was forming lavish, very lavish wedding plans in her mind, very satisfactory plans. One night in the midst of petting and kissing, Ilana casually mentioned the matter of a trust fund, whereupon Daniel casually replied that he had no trust fund. A shockwave disrupted the petting and kissing. By the next morning, the shockwave had reached Mrs. Alinski. The shockwave shattered Ilana's love for the nonexistent trust fund and Mrs. Alinski's equal love for the trust fund that did not exist. Her copious tears suggested, perhaps proved, that she had a greater love for the nonexistent fund than she had for her own daughter, who was, after all, much closer to the nonexistent fund than she was.

The shockwave engulfed Daniel as well, for he was truly in love, truly in love with an illusion, truly in love with a fantasy, truly in love with a hallucination. One's heart can be broken by a fantasy. One can pine at length after a hallucination. So it was with Daniel. The author cannot deny that Richard Melmont had mentioned the possibility of trust funds several times to Barbara and Daniel, but nothing along those lines had materialized.

Chapter Six

The Innocence of Barbara Melmont

Each righteous person has his own way of dealing with the world. Barbara Melmont went to law school to appease her father, but on her way to a degree, she was attracted to the Innocence Project, an attraction that her father considered counterproductive. You become a lawyer to make money, to become a partner in a prestigious law firm, and possibly help others, innocent or guilty, in the process. There was no money in the Innocence Project for a law student or a young attorney. There was just the chance of helping an innocent person wrongfully imprisoned for a crime he did not commit. The world is full of innocent people who suffer for one reason or another. What is the good of helping one person when there is a sea of people that you cannot help? Until the world is remade along different lines, helping one person out of seven billion is quixotic. For better or worse, Barbara had a conscience, the gene for which was missing in her father. Or perhaps he had the gene but it was suppressed by other genes that whispered to him self, self, self.

She took the small step of participating in an effort to exonerate an innocent man. A small step, certainly, compared with the tragedies that engulf the world, but one that made the world infinitesimally better rather than worse. How can an innocent man be found guilty by a court of law? Oh, it happens numerous times, usually to black men who enter the court under a cloud of suspicion.

The man in question was convicted of strangling a black prostitute to death and was sentenced to twenty-five years to life. A jogger saw him pull a body out of a gray car. He was wearing red jeans. Hair was found on the victim's body. Semen was found in her body. The "murderer" allegedly admitted to another prisoner that he did kill the woman.

But the jogger recanted. The confidant in jail confessed that he was lying. The red jeans did not fit. The hair samples were not his. A test performed several years later showed that the semen found in the woman's body was not his. His gray car was inoperable at the time of the murder and could not have been the car at the scene of the crime. It subsequently came out that the detective in charge of the case had committed seven murders on behalf of the Mafia.

After eight years of gathering all this evidence, real evidence, the court exonerated the "murderer," completely. After nineteen years in prison.

"I have permanent scars. It's a new world. I don't know anything about computers, cell phones, new kinds of cars. It's overwhelming."

Barbara Melmont and her colleagues were overwhelmed by moving the universe infinitesimally in the right direction through sheer force of facts.

New York City compensated the victim with a substantial amount of money to the extent that anyone can be compensated for nineteen lost years.

Conscience compensated Barbara and her colleagues with an ineffable feeling of righteousness.

Much of the world is innocent, Barbara thought. We have the facts to prove it. But we don't yet have an Innocence Project for the rest of the world.

Richard Melmont did not understand. He suffered from success in business, failure in the rest of life. His moral core was missing.

Chapter Seven

Barbara Melmont's Love

Jacob Rosen was a fellow law school student. Barbara easily persuaded him to join the Innocence Project, for something at the bottom of his soul hated injustice. The world as it is saddened him, the falling short of all the human possibilities that can be imagined but cannot be realized. Barbara and Jacob were likeminded and became friends. Then they became lovers. Richard Melmont did not approve. He did not approve of his daughter consorting with a Jew. He did not approve of his daughter consorting with a weak man, for if you do not have the strength to accept the world as it is you are weak. He did not approve of his daughter consorting with a socialist, for what could he be but a socialist if he was against everything?

He will amount to nothing. He will not get on in the world. You will pay the price for your idle dreams. So argued Richard Melmont with the conviction of certainty.

Have you forgotten the Sermon on the Mount? Those who work to heal the world are worth a great deal.

He is a Jew. He knows nothing of the Sermon on the Mount.

Surely a Jew can read, and read the Sermon on the Mount.

He is a socialist. He cares nothing for the Sermon on the Mount.

Jesus was a socialist. He cared a great deal for the Sermon on the Mount.

You are young and foolish. I trust that time and experience will dissipate these vapid thoughts.

So went conversations between father and daughter.

Father went so far as to arrange a dinner that included Barbara and a colleague, dropping a hint to his colleague that Barbara was available. This older gentleman was in want of a wife and was so bold and inept to say so to Barbara in the sitting room after dinner. He had many strong points. Money. An estate. A household staff. A group of influential friends who frequented his dinner table. He was but in want of a woman to administer this very satisfactory style of life. That is, he was in want of a wife. He made the offer as a business proposition, with the added advantage of great freedom for the wife and husband, who should not much interfere in each other's lives. What an attractive offer to a woman who seeks a business proposition! How could Barbara be polite in the face of such presumption? Should she be polite? She chose to be polite and say that she was otherwise engaged, and thank you for the generous offer. To which the presumptuous gentleman thanked her for her prompt response, no shillyshallying and nothing ventured nothing gained.

Jacob Rosen was a nondenominational socialist, if you must have a designation. He could find no party to suit him, only his vision of the world as it might be suited him. As a matter of fact, he was a nondenominational Jew as well. He was born into a Jewish family, but he did not have Jewish beliefs. He was neither an atheist nor an agnostic. He was greatly interested in the science of astrophysics and was content to agree with Einstein that the unresolved mysteries of the universe are what we call God. Which did not prevent him from taking Barbara to religious holidays celebrated by friends.

They were regular guests at the annual Passover dinner of his friends Conrad and Sarah O'Brian. How could Jews have the name O'Brian? Simple. When Conrad's grandfather came to the United States, he set out to find a job. And rather than use his actual name, Finkelman, he saw a billboard with the name O'Brian on his way to the interview, and so inspired, gave the name O'Brian in the interview. Not Abraham O'Brian either. Albert O'Brian. Who became the father of Kieran O'Brian, who became the father of Conrad O'Brian.

And so the Passover meal proceeded as written in the Haggadah. But when God was referred to as He, Jacob pointed out that we don't know if God is a He, She, or It, and we should just say God without a pronoun. A believing Jew replied that the traditional Haggadah always says He. In the ensuing argument, Jacob suggested a compromise in which the participants would say He on Mondays, Wednesdays, and Fridays, She on Tuesdays, Thursdays, and Saturdays, and It on Sunday. This so-called joke was taken in good humor, since friendship counted more than orthodoxy among those sitting around the table.

When someone recited the ten plagues that God inflicted on the Egyptians because Pharaoh would not let the Jews go, Jacob pointed out that a good God would not kill all the Egyptian first-born males because God does not punish the innocent. Not to mention the other nine plagues. Invariably someone said that the ways of God are mysterious to man, to which Jacob invariably replied that man blames his own evil ways on God. Furthermore, Passover never happened because there is no historical evidence that Jews lived in Egypt at the time in question. A fair-minded member of the group pointed out that many biblical stories are fables that give hope to later generations. Not just for Jews. For everyone.

Notwithstanding his contentiousness, Jacob willingly ate the bitter herbs, the charoset, and the matzah, and filled the cup with wine for Elijah, herald of the redeemer. When the time came for the children to look for the hidden matzah, each child found one to his or her delight, for Jacob always hid enough matzahs so that each child could find one and receive a new dollar bill as a reward.

Meanwhile Barbara became pregnant with a nondenominational socialist and she and Jacob went to a nondenominational justice of the peace and got married. Much to the exasperation of Richard Melmont and the pleasure of Maria and Daniel Melmont. But great-grandfather Melmont, who makes only a cameo appearance in this story, threatened on God's behalf that all the younger Melmonts would roast in hell if the forthcoming Melmont was not baptized.

Chapter Eight

A Day in the Life of Maria Melmont

Maria Melmont awakened on a bright spring morning, opened the curtains, and raised the sash. She took a deep breath of the fresh air, looked at the green lawn, the blue sky, and the white clouds. And she exclaimed, what a glorious day! Much to do today. Richard Melmont had invited guests for dinner to celebrate the launching of a bond traders' journal in which he had a financial interest. Maria would be the hostess. Much to do today. Also lunch with a college friend. But how can the beauty of this day be resisted? She would start out with a walk on the beach of the Long Island Sound, then have lunch, then go to an exhibit opening, then shop for flowers, and arrive at Richard's house in time to supervise the final arrangements for the dinner.

What was her life like with Richard, she mused as she tread along the beach. She had been attracted to his strength and single-mindedness. Whatever he put his hand to he had to succeed. He put his hand to making money. His imagination for making money was fertile. His imagination for implementing what he imagined was limitless. So much strength and single-mindedness to admire. But after a year or so it became evident that Richard lacked some other dimension possessed by most men, a sense of how others felt, a response to the way others felt. After the children had reached their early teens, it became evident that Richard's demanding, single-minded self was draining her, was preventing her from having a life of her own. She would not divorce him. She would continue to minister to him, but at some distance. She would establish her own residence. Money was not an issue. Richard wanted, needed, the propriety of a marriage, and so the matter was settled.

What if I had married Stephen, Maria wondered as she walked along the shore. They were lovers in college. He was brilliant. He was kind. She remembered how he had patiently initiated her into the mysteries of sex. He had wanted to marry her, but she hesitated. Then she had wanted to marry him and he hesitated. The opportunity passed. That was unfortunate. Several years later, when they both were at the beginning of their professional lives, Stephen as a biologist and she as a writer, he called out of the blue and said, let's get married. Oh my Lord, I had just agreed to marry someone else, that someone else being Richard Melmont. What would life have been like if he had called a month earlier? I still love everyone I ever loved, she thought.

Maria bought flowers on her way home and put them in a vase to keep them fresh until evening. On her way to lunch at noon she met Severn on the street. Severn was Julie French's husband, the very woman she was about to meet for lunch. How are you, Severn? Severn was distracted and stared at Maria, then shook his inner self and said hello, I'm all right. Severn was not all right. He had returned from Iraq and was not the man that Julie had married. He was preoccupied, irritable, unable to resume his job as manager of a shopping mall in the suburbs.

Maria arrived at lunch quite shaken and could not get off the subject of Severn. Julie was shaken as well, distraught, because Severn continued to live in another world, a world in which he had defiled his inner self, and had killed people. Only once did he speak about it, then he could not speak about it again, not to Julie, not to his brother, not to his therapist, not to his minister, to no one. He had been at a checkpoint. A car approached. The driver did not stop. The driver did not respond to frantic armwaving. At the last second Severn fired and the car careened off the road and crashed into the side of a warehouse. Severn pulled out a man, a woman, a young girl, and a young boy. They were all dead. Severn went into shock and was hospitalized and heavily sedated. No, he was not the same man when he came home. He woke up in the night with a loud cry. He saw the family in the car passing in the street during the day. He was going to therapy sessions with other veterans whose moral selves had been violated. An author was invited to attend the sessions. Some spoke. Some wrote stories. Some wrote poems. Some sat mute and listened.

This was not the lunch that Maria and Julia had planned.

Maria thought of her father as she drove to the art gallery for the opening. He never went through such extreme stress as Severn. He went through a different kind of stress. After he left college, he marched from Montgomery to Selma to end segregation in the South when truncheoning the marchers was still acceptable. He demonstrated outside the White House to end the Vietnam War when demonstrating was still unpopular. Then her thoughts contrasted three men. Her husband, self-absorbed. Her father and Severn, in their different ways possessing an inner moral core. Severn crushed by an involuntary act of violence. Her father sustained in voluntary acts of solidarity.

Maria's mother-in-law lived in Grosvenor Square most of the year. She had an interest in the art gallery in Greenwich to which Maria now made her way. Her motive was simply to keep peace between herself and her mother-in-law. This was an impossible mission. The senior Mrs. Melmont had not liked Maria from the start, whom she deemed not socially suitable for her son. A member of the British nobility would have been more to her liking. Or some equivalent woman from the American aristocracy. She clearly perceived that there was an American aristocracy, popular belief to the contrary notwithstanding. At this point she also believed that all the younger Melmonts would roast in hell if the forthcoming child was not baptized, but only believed it metaphorically. Maria did not have much interest in the actual exhibit of abstract art. One five-foot cube of spiky wire was called Past, Present, and Future, but each part looked the same as every other part. Apparently the artist believed that the past, present, and future were one undistinguishable jumble.

Maria arrived promptly at six to preside over Richard's dinner party.

Chapter Nine

Richard Melmont

Richard Melmont adhered to a strict schedule. He went to bed at midnight and awoke at seven. He slept deeply and had no dreams, none that he could remember. At seven-thirty he went to his exercise room and worked out for half an hour. At eight he showered then went to the dining room for breakfast. At eight forty-five he boarded his helicopter and was flown to a helipad in Manhattan.

Today he thought about his past, his difficult life. His grandparents emigrated from Volgograd, formerly Stalingrad, survivors of The Great Patriotic War, as the Russians called it. They too changed their name when they arrived in America, from Melgora—literally Chalk Mountain—to Melmont. Ah, America! To breath freely, to go where you wished, to speak your mind without fear. Heaven on Earth. Grandfather was a talented goldsmith and built up a thriving business. He was about to sign a contract with Macy's when he died of pneumonia as a result of standing in freezing rain waiting for a bus. Grandmother went mad, closed all the windows of their apartment, stuffed towels under the door, turned on the gas stove, and lined up her two sons and two daughters, aged six, four, three, and one. Then the baby began to cry. Grandmother picked him up. That broke the spell. Grandmother turned off the gas.

Grandmother was a Jew, so, thought Richard Melmont, she was clever in business. She opened a general store and thrived. Richard particularly remembered the story about a drunk who regularly came to the store for a handout. One time he fell down the basement stairs and lay there. Grandmother feared going down. She stood at the top of the stairs holding a glass in her hand that she somehow implied was schnapps. The inebriated man slowly shambled up the stairs and reached for the glass expecting a drink. It was a drink. A drink of water.

Richard's mother converted to Episcopalianism to avoid the vestiges of anti-Semitism and to marry up, high up. Richard thought about his brief time at Sunday school. His temper already manifested itself. A teacher reprimanded him for failing to do his homework. Young Richard picked up a protractor that he was using to draw a cross and hurled it at the teacher, inflicting a gash in her cheek. He was expelled.

Richard then thought about his difficult life with Maria and their children. Maria was an elegant, attractive, dignified woman. He had envisioned a partnership. But she wanted some kind of love, intimacy, affection that he could not give. Some kind of merger of souls, of spirits, of thought. He remembered a woman who had no such needs or desires. She wanted to preside, be a gracious lady, a cynosure to all eyes. Had he not taken a wrong turn when he parted from this woman, for reasons that he could not even remember? Had he not taken a wrong turn when he married Maria, who wanted to be great, but also wanted something intangible, something beyond his imagination? And the children. Oh, the children. So demanding. At five little Daniel wanted spinach for dinner, lots of spinach, mountains of spinach. Popeye, you know, became superstrong when he ate spinach. Maria served spinach. More, more, more, a mountain of spinach on Daniel's plate. Oh, he hated it at the first taste. Melmont thought back. I demanded that Daniel eat the spinach. All the spinach. Daniel had *demanded* spinach. More, more, more. So he must eat the spinach. Daniel climbed off his chair in fear of my anger and hid under the table. Mother said, all right. Let him alone. Let him not eat the spinach. This indulgence made me furious. In a moment of uncontrollable rage I grabbed my glass and hurled the water at Maria.

For a long time my daughter Barbara did not speak to me. For a long time Daniel suffered from fear, of me, even fear of a person passing in a car who simply looked at him, or of a receptionist in a doctor's office who asked him a perfectly innocent question. By sheer logic and will, he eventually managed to reason himself out of this frightful reflex.

Then as we were approaching Manhattan, I remembered an elderly uncle with a Russian accent who sat in the alleyway behind my grandmother's house—she could now afford a house—reading. He was always reading Spinoza, marking passages. My uncle was a scholar, an old, poor, penniless scholar. He believed with Spinoza that God and the universe were one. I always handed him a few dollars as I teased this Jew for his eternal interest in Spinoza, God, and the universe.

After landing at the helipad and heading for the financial district, I remembered the story of a very prominent young banker whom I much admired. He was an avid flyer and owned a one-engine Cessna. He regularly flew his son to summer camp in the Berkshires. After he dropped his son off the last time, he flew some loops over the camp for the amazement and enjoyment of the campers and counselors. But he miscalculated, or the engine malfunctioned, or a downdraft swept in, and he crashed and killed himself. I have never gotten over it, not in thirty years. His wife and son were crazed with grief. After a few months, aside from their inconsolable suffering, they realized that the financial support for the family was suddenly gone. I decided to take it upon myself to maintain their standard of living and send the son to college. Nobody can say that I have no feelings.

Well, I'm in my office now and here's how I run my business. First, facts, facts, facts. Data, data, data. Information, information, information. I have offices in London, Paris, Zurich, Milan, Moscow, Dubai, and Hong Kong. Every one of my investment staff must succeed or they are no longer a member of my investment staff. I do not deal in sentiment. I deal in investments. I deal in success. No, I do not deal in greed. I do not think that greed is good. I think that accepting the world as it is, is good, is necessary, has no alternative. I act accordingly.

Chapter Ten

A Visit to Melmont Investments

Richard Melmont finally prevailed on Barbara to work in the legal department of Melmont Investments. She was, after all, his daughter, and he offered her the opportunity to see the workings of a really great investment house. Really great in size, shall we say. He offered to make a large contribution to the Innocence Project as part of her compensation, although the project was so small it is hard to say what it would do with a sizable contribution. Then again, maybe the work of Melmont Investments produced some social benefit that she hadn't perceived. Or maybe not. Whatever the case, she would not work on military contracts.

Melmont had bought a large share of Schott Paper, a share large enough to persuade the directors to appoint him CEO. The author thinks the name was Schott Paper, but the reputation for authorial omniscience is highly overrated. Schott Paper, if that's the name, had a plant outside of Philadelphia and was the second largest manufacturer of paper products in the world. Before Richard Melmont arrived, management had made some bad investments, which caused the stock price to fall precipitously. Melmont saw a clear way to turn the company around. He divested Schott Paper of all its poor investments, closed the main plant outside of Philadelphia, fired five thousand employees, and moved production to a small site in Boca Raton, which, incidentally, means mouse's mouth. By then Melmont had whittled down Schott Paper to the manufacture of its best product, for which it was widely known: toilet paper. The share price shot up, at which time Melmont sold the company to another producer of paper goods, Kim-Clarkson, put on his golden parachute, and left Schott Paper with one hundred million dollars in addition to the gains from his stock, which sold at the highest price on record. After all, Schott still made the best toilet paper.

Richard Melmont had destroyed a company, which continued to exist in name only within Kim-Clarkson, had fired five thousand people, shut down fifty-one warehouses which removed another five thousand people from the payroll, had removed a valuable asset from greater Philadelphia, had incurred the wrath of thousands of bankrupt shopkeepers and their families who had served the fired workers and their families, and walked away with what is often called a cool hundred million.

At which point Richard Melmont gained the sobriquet Sledgehammer Dick, both in the press, on TV, on the Internet, and in polite conversation.

At which point Barbara Melmont left her job.

Chapter Eleven

Titans Fall Out

It's one thing to deceive unwary members of the public. It's quite another to deceive your own colleagues. The management of Moonbeam Products, a manufacturer of coffee makers, blenders, toasters, microwave ovens, and other kitchen appliances, had also overextended into collateral fields and its share price had plummeted. Richard Melmont again bought stock at bargain prices and became chairman of the board of directors. He persuaded the five other controlling directors to sell off the recently acquired unprofitable companies, close twelve Moonbeam plants, and fire several thousand employees. Moonbeam stock shot up, but Melmont couldn't find a buyer. To keep the stock prices up, he convinced the board to buy a controlling share of a profitable company called Outdoor Equipment, quite a stretch for a manufacturer of kitchen appliances. The deal looked good but turned out to be not as good as it looked. Melmont began to sell camping gear to retailers at unheard-of discounts, encouraging them to buy now and pay later. Melmont convinced the Moonbeam accounting office to book the sales immediately even though the deal was "buy now, pay later." The apparent revenue of Moonbeam shot up. But then financial experts in camping goods noticed that a tremendous number of items like barbeque grills were piling up in warehouses off season, which never could be sold when the season for barbeque grills arrived. The price of Moonbeam shares fell close to zero.

A stormy board meeting ensued. Accusations flew. Screwed your own partners, you bastard. No values, no honor. No loyalty, no ethics.

After four days of raging, handwringing, and tears, Melmont quit.

That was the moment when Melmont lost his family.

Daniel Melmont was quoted as saying, he even cheated his partners. I told him Moonbeam would ruin him.

Barbara Melmont was quoted as saying, it's maddening, he deserved it.

Such remarks were reported in the tabloid press. True or not, it's hard to say.

Maria Melmont was silent.

Richard Melmont did not get what he deserved. He had sold Moonbeam stock at its highest point and walked away with several hundred million.

The sobriquet Sledgehammer Dick stuck.

Chapter Twelve

Another Unpleasant Encounter

George Banat was one of the board members of Moonbeam who had been swindled by Richard Melmont, along with thousands of trusting investors. Banat's loss was staggering by ordinary standards, but ordinary standards didn't apply. Banat was one of the wealthiest men in the world. A large loss to someone else was a small loss to him, but nevertheless it stung. He usually made the right moves at the right time, but this time he had been swindled. He did not make a wrong guess about the market. He was deceived, outright lied to, and he seethed with contempt for Melmont.

George Banat was originally named Georgi Benyamin, born in Budapest in 1930. At fourteen, the Jewish Council, an organization set up by the Nazis to carry out anti-Jewish measures, assigned Georgi the task of listing all the Jewish shopkeepers in his neighborhood. Benyamin senior warned him that everyone on the list would be deported to concentration camps. His father changed the family name to Banat to dodge the sting of anti-Semitism. Banat, by the way, is a region in the south of Hungary, a very Hungarian name. The family fled Budapest one step ahead of the Nazis. First they went to Geneva, then they went to London, where Georgi became George and attended the London School of Economics. He joined a medium-sized banking firm where he became a currency trader. Then through contacts in New York, he emigrated to the United States where he started his own currency trading company, which grew as a result of his sheer brilliance in anticipating currency fluctuations. His biggest opportunity came when he realized that the British pound was overvalued. Business was sluggish, housing was overpriced, and exports were declining. A devaluation of the pound was inevitable. But the Chancellor of the Exchequer stubbornly refused to devalue the pound out of some kind of long-tarnished imperial pride together with gross ignorance of economics. Banat borrowed ten billion dollars' worth of pounds from several currency brokers, paid the usual fees, immediately sold the pounds at the inflated price, and waited for the pound to sink to a lower price relative to other currencies. Finally even the Chancellor of the Exchequer realized that he had no choice and devalued the pound. Whereupon Banat bought ten billion dollars' worth of pounds at the lower price, returned the borrowed pounds to the broker, and pocketed one billion dollars, the difference between the higher and lower prices. In technical language, he sold short. That transaction made Banat a very wealthy man. Subsequent transactions put him on the *Forbes* 400 list of richest persons in the world. He is quoted as saying that he gets terrible backaches when something is not quite right, and he is forced to reexamine his strategy to get rid of the backache. Evidently he did not get a backache during the Moonbeam caper.

Banat was also a man with a conscience. He played the game as the world had set up the game. But he also felt an obligation to return something to society. He set up the Free Society Forum and gave billions to institutes in Russia, Central Europe, and Africa to promote movements dedicated to free societies. He was a force for good to the extent that any private person can be a force for good, knowing full well that no well-intentioned person can ever be a match for ill-intentioned governments.

Shortly after the Moonbeam fiasco, the socially prominent Dolly Nosegay, Maria's friend from several book clubs back, arranged a small dinner party to celebrate the graduation of her daughter Margaret from high school. Not knowing of the bad blood between George Banat and Richard Melmont, she had invited them both, along with Maria, Barbara, and Daniel Melmont. When Banat and Melmont sat down to dinner, insults began to fly back and forth, to the consternation of the other guests and the mortification of Dolly Nosegay.

You are a thief.

You are a thief.

You are dishonest.

You are naïve.

A most unpleasant dinner was finally over, and the two men were escorted to different ends of the parlor with apprehensive guests trying to deflect their animosity by talking about the weather, the latest play, or the most recent trip to Bermuda. Melmont would not be appeased. He charged toward Banat. Young Margaret Nosegay impulsively threw open the front door and yelled, Police! Police! Daniel Melmont grabbed his advancing father by the wrists, and being bigger, younger, and more muscular, held him in place. Dolly Nosegay assured her daughter that the police were not needed, please don't make a public spectacle, come in and close the door. The guests left. The Melmonts left. Banat left. Dolly Nosegay repeatedly asked no one, What have I done? What have I done? Margaret Nosegay assured her, Nothing, mother. You have done nothing. They were both quaking.

Chapter Thirteen

Severn Is Healed

Severn is not doing well. The scene at the checkpoint repeats itself in his head. He cannot speak about it. The family in the car was middle class, the father, mother, and children well-dressed, probably driving to a safer location, probably not understanding the signs to stop, probably disconcerted by the wild waving of arms as the father failed to slow down. He didn't understand. But for an instant the family lives on. There was no consolation in talking. There was no consolation in books. There was no consolation in music. He played Schubert's *An die Musik* in his head. Du holde Kunst . . . Thou noble Art . . . How in his past life that music and those words had pierced him. But now the feeling flies away from him and he flies after it as if to catch the evanescent, the uncatchable. Then he thought of the words, do not go gentle into that good night . . . The struggle not to go gentle into that good night, that struggle, that struggle, that struggle—is killing *him*. Then he thought of the words, a time to kill, and a time to heal; a time to break down, and a time to build up . . . A time to kill is killing *him*, killing *him*, killing *him*. A time to heal has vanished. No time to build up, no time to build up. He heard the consoling words. He heard the consoling music. Words of no consolation. Music of no consolation. Desolate words. Desolate music. And what of the words, thou shalt not kill, thou shalt not kill, thou shalt not kill? And what of the words thou *shalt* kill, thou *shalt* kill, thou *shalt* kill? And what of the words, a time to kill and a time to heal, to kill and to heal, to kill and to heal? The motor of the car was running in the garage and the doors of the garage were closed and Severn sat at the steering wheel healed forever.

Chapter Fourteen

The Stevens Family at Home

John Stevens was a tall, thin, muscular man in his early eighties. He had worked for Richard Melmont for some twenty-five years, loyally, efficiently, intelligently. He went out of his way to avoid conflict with any member of the Melmont family, no matter what he thought personally. He was no ordinary estate manager, if there was such a person. He was born into the upper middle class and had gotten a degree in business administration at the Wharton School. You might ask why he settled for a job as an estate manager. He had not settled for a job. As a student, he took a great interest in historical estates, their architecture, their management, their location, and their fate. Some old estates have been well maintained up to this day. Others have decayed or have been torn down to make way for clusters of smaller houses. John Stevens regarded estate management as a profession in the same sense as managing any other business. He knew that he could restore the demolished foyer in a matter of days because he had read that a similar feat had been accomplished in an old mansion in Charleston after the first floor had been gutted by a hurricane. The owner had expected to entertain a member of British royalty. The caretaker and a landscape designer set everything to rights in a matter of days and the royal personage was welcomed as if nothing had happened.

John Stevens reminisced about his father who had gone to Jefferson Medical College and graduated just in time to be drafted into the army as a second lieutenant when the United States joined the Allies in the Great War. He was shipped to Brest, France, as far away as you could get from the fighting, and was among the first generation of doctors to learn to take x-rays of the human body. When he returned to Philadelphia and opened a practice, he found the medical profession skeptical. What is the good of radiology? Then one day the mayor of Philadelphia was shot in the shoulder and the surgeons could not locate the bullet. Dr. Stevens was called in. He took some x-rays and pointed to the bullet shown on several films clipped up in his light boxes. The surgeons removed the bullet, the mayor recovered, and this amazing new radiology was accepted as an indispensible diagnostic device. Stevens always remembered this story with the pleasure of a son who is proud of his father.

The young John Stevens grew up during the Depression, but he saw the Depression from the perch of an upper-middle-class family, living in a large upper-middle-class house on a tree-lined street in an upper-middle-class neighborhood. For some inexplicable reason, maybe it was in the genes, he suffered from the hardship that he saw around him. At eight he walked through a nearby ghetto. The shacks were falling down. The children were in rags. They played in the dirt around the shacks. His father employed a series of homeless men to wash the car, mow the lawn, shovel the snow, and drive his mother on errands. Each in turn lived in a makeshift basement room next to the furnace. A white man named Bill staggered home on weekends stinking drunk. A black man named Charlie was next in succession, and he was dignified, intelligent, and sober. Later in life, John Stevens thought, what a waste. Under different circumstances Charlie could have been a doctor, a lawyer, or a professor. Next came another black man named Jim. Young John Stevens' last recollection of Jim was seeing him in a hospital bed with welts all over his body. He died the following day. In a different world, all these men would have led different lives.

The mature John Stevens had a family of his own. His wife Naomi worked as managing editor of a glossy magazine of fashion and opinion. Their two teenaged daughters lived with them in a cottage on the Richard Belmont estate. As children, Barbara and Daniel were always welcome, always invited to holiday parties, received boisterously with spirited hugs and kisses. Both Naomi and John came from large families. On holidays the cottage was packed with relatives and friends. The intermarried black and white relatives were welcomed. The intermarried white and Latino relatives were welcomed. The black and Latino relatives were welcomed. As were their friends. The food was always a multicultural feast. On Christmas Day, John Stevens presided, asking each in turn what they wished for, gave a speech about memories of good times together and anticipation of good times to come, and then assigned groups of four or five guests to sing each repetition of the Twelve Days of Christmas. Each group sang out in turn: 12 Drummers Drumming, 11 Pipers Piping, 10 Lords a-Leaping, 9 Ladies Dancing, 8 Maids a-Milking, 7 Swans a-Swimming, 6 Geese a-Laying, 5 Golden Rings, 4 Calling Birds, 3 French Hens, 2 Turtle Doves, and a Partridge in a Pear Tree. The scene was uproarious.

The boisterous Stevens household contrasted with the sedate Melmont household. The young Barbara and Daniel took note and cogitated.

Richard Melmont expressed a particular interest in the Stevens' daughters, Sarah and Daisy. He offered Sarah a job in the mansion as a kind of social secretary. Not an onerous job. He made a point of having her with him when he worked in his study. He gave her a significant bonus at Christmas time.

He offered to take her on business trips, which she declined. At one time he advanced to touch her hair, upon which she turned and left the room, and left the house, and left the job. John and Naomi Stevens had been suspicious of all this attention. Soon Sarah moved out of her parental home, rented an apartment in New York, and found a job as social secretary to a dowager who was interested in the arts.

What would John Stevens do or say? Nothing. He continued in his punctilious way of managing the estate, directing the staff, ordering the supplies, and dealing with contingencies. All this with a new understanding of Richard Melmont and a well-concealed contempt. Naomi Stevens shared her husband's feelings, along with a better understanding of the unenviable position in which Maria Melmont found herself.

Chapter Fifteen

A Conversation Between an Old Bolshevik and a Young African American

Two friends of the Stevens, Dmitri Mikhailovich Belinsky and Ralph Laurel Crosby, sat in a quiet alcove during the holiday party and talked. Dmitri Mikhailovich had been a prisoner in the Soviet Gulag in the 1950s. Ralph Crosby had been in an American prison in the 1990s. They were comparing notes.

Dmitiri had been a Communist commissioned as a captain during World War II. Early in the war his unit was surrounded by the Nazis and he was taken prisoner. After six months he and four other Russian prisoners managed to escape and return to the front line. Three of the five were shot to death as they approached the Soviet side. Dmitri and one comrade managed to cross the front and survived. The secret police immediately suspected them of being German spies, for who could escape from a German prison camp? The two were shipped off to the Gulag, notwithstanding the fact that Dmitri had been a loyal Communist and his comrade had risked his life in defense of the Soviet homeland.

The Gulag was an archipelago of camps spread across barren land in Siberia. In winter, temperatures were as much as forty degrees below zero, sometimes more. The prisoners were treated as traitors, army traitors, party traitors, intellectual traitors, worker traitors. The merest suspicion could land a man in the Gulag. Even less than a suspicion. A deliberately unfounded accusation could result in arrest and unremitting labor for a year, ten years, twenty years, and more.

First the prisoners had to contend with the biting cold and perpetual frost against which ragged clothing, boots, mittens, and caps were completely inadequate. They were forced to work until the temperature fell below minus forty-two degrees Fahrenheit. Then they scrambled for the slop, or what was called food rations. The ability to hide a little extra slop was very heaven. Or to be a good friend of the cook. Then the unremitting work from dawn to dusk. Then the crowding in bunks with soiled blankets. Then the stink of the pails of urine and feces that were carried out of the barracks and dumped on the frost-covered ground every day. Then the punishment of extra work and less slop for the slightest infraction of the rules. Each day of freezing, hunger, and backbreaking work was no different from any other day. A package of food and clothing might come from a relative every few months. That was a cause for rejoicing. Maybe sometime in the future the day of release would arrive, but the *zek*, the prisoner, would always be a marked man, an offender for just mentioning the inhuman conditions of the Gulag to anyone unless whispered to trusted family members or friends. But who knew who could be trusted? Then when Nikita Khrushchev allowed Alexander Solzhenitsyn to publish *One Day in the Life of Ivan Denisovich,* the pall lifted and the Soviet public was horrified to learn the truth about what it had always suspected. But, said Dmitri Mikhailovich, the pall will never lift from my consciousness, my feelings, my memories. I will go to my grave carrying the pain of the Gulag in my soul.

Then Ralph Crosby told his story. You've had your crime and punishment, I've had mine. You are out of your Gulag. I'm still in mine. I was an innocent kid growing up in Harlem. My mother worked at a nursing home spoon-feeding old white ladies and changing their diapers. I went to school, I sang in the church choir, I took trumpet lessons so I could play like Louis Armstrong. When I was sixteen I started to hang out with a gang in my neighborhood. They all did crack. So I started doing crack and I got hooked. We all ran away from the cops, but one day a cop stopped me and I had to turn out my pockets and he found a trace of crack. I got a year and probation. I got out and my preacher said, be responsible. I wanted to be responsible, but how? I asked him, how? I can't get off the habit. So I ran into a cop again and got arrested again, and got sent up again, this time for five years. Man, if you're not already a criminal, prison is the best place to make you one. A lifer came at me with a knife. If some of the younger guys hadn't backed him off I'd be dead. I had nightmares about being locked up in solitary. I yelled but nobody heard me. Then I woke up. I dreamed that Jesus walked into my cell. I held out my hand, then he turned his back and walked away. I can't get a job when I get out. The name "criminal" hangs around my neck. I can't finish school. I can't start a family. I have to report to a parole officer, which means I'm still in the "system." One more stop and search and I'm in for twenty-five years to life. Three strikes and you're out, which means in. Why do I have to live like this because I got hooked on crack when I was sixteen years old? I didn't commit a crime. An ounce of crack when I was a kid, no freedom for the rest of my life, in or out. What sense does that make? Ten years gone by. Still in the "system." Next time, three strikes and *I'm* out, white guys mostly passed by. Whose life is worse, yours or mine?

The party got boisterous again and the author could not hear the rest of the conversation.

Chapter Sixteen

The Cure

The problems with Richard propelled Maria into the realm of fantasy, not unusual for a writer of fiction. Her problems merged with the problems of the world and she began to fantasize about a pill, yes, a wonderful pill that would solve the problems of the world, hers included. Let's say that this pill would alter the chemistry in the brain and suppress the urge to act pathologically, against the interests of others. Or suppress the action of the aggressive genes, or result in some wonderful process that would cause everyone to act altruistically. She wasn't writing as a physiologist but as a fantasist. But, she told herself, if there are biochemical differences in the brains of altruists and psychopaths, why can't the brain biochemistry of the psychopaths be altered for the good? No. Too far-fetched. The reading public would laugh in her face if the story got so far as being published. No publisher in his right mind would publish such a story.

It happens that Maria Melmont and Naomi Stevens were on friendly terms and spoke on the phone occasionally. Naomi Stevens, you remember, was the manager of a magazine directed to wealthy upper-class readers interested in travel, fashion, art, and elegance in all aspects of life. In addition to articles on these subjects, the magazine carried opinion pieces by highly regarded authors on social issues. This relatively new magazine was modeled on a relatively new Russian magazine called *Snob*, designed to be read by wealthy Russians who were also interested in travel, fashion, art, and elegance, the soigné Russians. *Snob* is the same word in Russian as in English, a word used as a wink to the cognoscenti. English, of course, is much more widely spoken around the world than Russian. The publishers of the English-language magazine expected to do much better than *Snob.* As another wink to the congnoscenti, they called their magazine *Slob,* confident that the upper-class English-language readers would appreciate the inversion.

Getting back to Maria Melmont's idea for a story, she mentioned it to Naomi Stevens, who, to Maria's surprise, not only thought the idea a good subject for a story, but promised to urge the editors of *Slob* to publish it. It happened that Naomi had come across an article about brain research in which the researchers were investigating the possibility of developing a "morality pill" just as Maria was fantasizing. So the idea wasn't far-fetched after all.

Maria sat down in front of her computer and opened a Word document.

The Cure

A husband and wife team of biochemists thought that they were on to something. They had been studying pairs of caged rats. One had access to chocolate while the other was trapped in a tube that could only be opened from the outside. Most rats that had access to the chocolate freed the trapped rats and shared the chocolate. Almost a third did not. The two biochemists experimented with a long series of brain-altering drugs and on their eighty-fifth trial found one that altered the brain chemistry of the selfish rats. All the rats that had access to the chocolate then freed their trapped mates and shared the chocolate with them. In subsequent experiments on other animals, the husband and wife team obtained the same results. They then applied to the Food and Drug Administration to do a limited experiment on humans.

With F.D.A. approval, they selected several hundred volunteers with diverse backgrounds, who were compensated for their time. The first group of volunteers played cards. About 10 percent cheated. This group was asked to take "pill 85"—it was not identified as the morality pill as such to the volunteers. Amazingly this group stopped cheating after they had taken the pill.

Then the husband and wife team arranged for a second group to shop for a tube of toothpaste at a pharmacy, giving them each a $20 bill for which they must get change. The clerk was instructed to give each volunteer $100 extra in change. About 10 percent kept the $100 while the rest pointed out to the clerk that he had made a mistake. Then the 10 percent took "pill 85" and returned the excess change that they had taken. Finally the remaining volunteers were divided into 10 groups and each group was asked to appear at a meeting precisely at a given hour. If they were late, they would be dropped from the experiment. In a corridor on the way to the meeting room, a woman lay on the floor pretending to be in pain. Out of each group of 10 volunteers, nine stopped to help the woman in spite of the prospect of being dropped from the experiment. Several weeks later, a similar experiment was arranged in which two children in the corridor were pretending to do bodily harm to each other. The 10 percent who had not stopped to help the woman on the floor had been given "pill 85" and this time they stopped to calm down the children.

The researchers were elated. They asked the F.D.A. for permission to experiment with 1,000 volunteers. The F.D.A. agreed. The results were spectacular.

The time came for the F.D.A. to approve the morality pill, which would be dispensed with a doctor's prescription. But they hesitated. What would the Secretary of Defense have to say about the morality pill? What would politicians who misled the public have to say? What would bankers who misled investors have to say? What would happen if the pill were approved for use in the United States but not in Russia, China, or Iran?

Most of the brain research community agreed that the morality pill would induce those who swallowed it to act altruistically but would not prevent them from responding appropriately to those who acted aggressively.

A great national discussion ensued, which soon spread around the world. In small experiments, prisoners and guards began to treat each other humanely. Managers of super PACs resigned. Inside traders stopped trading. Tea Party members started supporting Social Security. Soldiers in certain countries stopped shooting demonstrators. Terrorists put away their bombs and embraced Martin Luther King Jr. as their hero.

Soon an international conference was called to discuss a treaty to require everyone in the world to take the morality pill. The leaders of every country in the world agreed except for one holdout. That country was—

Just then the phone rang. It was Naomi asking Maria how she was coming along with the story. Just fine, she said. I'm almost finished. She then told Naomi the gist of the tale. Naomi assured Maria that *Slob* would almost certainly publish it.

Chapter Seventeen

Some Good News

Reader, we need something pleasant to report, and we have it. You recall that a wealthy banker friend of Richard Melmont was in want of a wife to manage his social life. Ilana Alenski was in want of a husband with a trust fund in order to find a secure position in the upper reaches of our national aristocracy. Through the grapevine they heard of each other. We are said to have six degrees of separation on the larger grapevine, but on the smaller branch of the grapevine about which we are speaking, the degree of separation is on the order of two. Maria Melmont arranged a small dinner party, with considerable reservations about such doings, but with no wish to stand between two would-be lovers, or at least two individuals who were thinking of marrying each other, sight unseen. Upon actually seeing each other at the dinner, both sides of the would-be couple found the other acceptable, notwithstanding the fact that our banker friend was thirty years Ilana's senior. At the appropriate moment, when the two could go off to a corner for a private conversation, drinks in hand, the matter of matrimony was discussed and an amicable agreement was arrived at.

Ilana was not to marry a trust fund after all, but a very wealthy banker. A prenup limiting her to ten million dollars in case of divorce was quite acceptable. The deal, business deal, shall we say, was consummated within half an hour's discussion and the couple returned to the throng of guests to announce the good news. As you would expect, there was much clinking of glasses and well-wishing.

Later that evening, Isabelle Alenski, although not in the least astonished, became a very gratified mother when she received a call from her daughter. On subsequent days, one could not help but notice that her head was held higher than the usual way heads are held.

Chapter Eighteen

Executive Session of the Senate Armed Services Committee

Richard Melmont was invited to testify before a closed session of the Senate Armed Services Committee. He was on a first-name basis with all the senators present since he was heavily invested in arms production and had testified several times before. After pleasantries were exchanged, the meeting was called to order and Melmont explained the coordinated research being conducted at his laboratories in France and the United States. Briefly, his leading nuclear physicists were on the verge of a breakthrough that would allow them to cause an instantaneous transitional intensification of dark energy, the intangible stuff that permeates all space. A transitional intensification would vaporize all protoplasm within the affected area but would leave all other physical objects intact. From a military point of view, every living thing in the affected area would be killed but property would not be destroyed. The advantages were obvious. No postwar reconstruction would be necessary. The cost savings would be enormous. The extent of protoplasmic destruction could be focused on areas varying from half a mile to several hundred miles in radius. Protoplasmic destruction was a term used by the researchers as a euphemism for killing people.

The committee members immediately recognized this as serious business, extremely serious business. What happens if the U.S. government supports this research? What happens if the U.S. government does not support this research? Can we stop information on the DEP, that is, the Dark Energy Project, from leaking? What happens if another government succeeds in harnessing dark energy first? Should we immediately seek an international treaty to ban all research on harnessing dark energy? All the "what ifs" were intensely discussed. The senators agreed that we had better be first, we had better be in a position of strength when it comes to negotiating, we had better be several years ahead of any possible rivals. At last a weapons system would emerge to eliminate all wars! The Defense Department must immediately allocate funds to support Dark Energy Systems, the name of Richard Melmont's enterprise, the name of this particular enterprise among his many enterprises. An initial funding of three billion dollars was mentioned.

A collateral discussion arose among the committee members. All had been made aware of the explosion at Melmont's estate. Could a foreign government have planted a mole in the C.I.A. to investigate Dark Energy Systems and take out its guiding genius? Could some scientist in Melmont's inner circle have become stricken with guilt and wished to kill Melmont? Could information have been leaked to a pacifist group? The entire discussion was speculation and went nowhere.

On both these issues, one senator held his peace.

Chapter Nineteen

Richard Melmont's Super PAC

Richard Melmont had wide support for Dark Energy Systems from the outset. Members of the Senate Armed Services Committee immediately spoke to the Secretary of Defense, the undersecretaries, and the assistant secretaries. Each from his own vantage point saw the need to proceed, be the first, get the job done quickly. The president was briefed. Several billion dollars must be allocated from Defense Department funds to complete the research and construct a working model of the dark energy weapons system.

Nevertheless Melmont wished to leave nothing to chance. His super PAC legally allowed him to contribute large sums of money from the coffers of Melmont Investments to advocate government support for the project and to place a time limit on its completion. Melmont Investments regularly retained K Street Advocates to deploy lobbyists, in this case to disseminate convincing reasons why Dark Energy Systems was public spirited and in this case essential for national defense. In these endeavors K Street Advocates invariably succeeded in convincing those who needed to be convinced. Trips to meetings in Palm Beach, Las Vegas, London, Paris, and Qatar, sponsored and paid for by Melmont Investments, were invariably necessary for those who needed to know the facts, including members of the press. K Street Advocates produced a glossy brochure about the exciting peacetime uses of dark energy with an obscure hint that dark energy might have military uses as well.

Perhaps Richard Melmont's most persuasive method of gathering support for his numerous schemes was to whisper in the ear of a senator, congressman, a member of the administration, or an influential banker at the time that the initial public offering was made, that now was the time to purchase shares in Dark Energy Systems, for the share price would surely rise. One of Melmont's frequent sayings was that all trading was insider trading, and the rest was a lottery. It followed that only insiders could engage in insider trading. What could be more obvious?

How could such a large undertaking as Dark Energy Systems be kept secret? It could not be. Three months after the closed-door hearing of the Senate Armed Services Committee, the *Washington Post* published a front-page article written by a well-known investigative journalist with inside connections giving a full account of Dark Energy Systems. The ongoing research in France and the United States, the closed-door hearing, the activities of the super PAC, the all-out support of high-level officials and bankers, the surge in stock purchases of Dark Energy Systems by knowledgeable individuals, all led to the concluding section of the article: Do these people know what they are doing?

By the next day, the *New York Times*, the *Boston Globe*, the *Los Angeles Times*, the *Chicago Tribune*, MSNBC, Fox News, CNN, the Huffington Post, and every newspaper, TV channel, and public affairs blog were humming with a new new sensational story, which in this case was actually sensational. At the same time the price of stock in Dark Energy Systems rose dramatically.

Chapter Twenty

A Family Confrontation

Maria, Barbara, Daniel, and Jacob recoiled from the dark energy plan. So many things could go wrong. What if everything went right and a dark energy weapon was finally produced? Would it lead to world peace or world war? No one could pierce the darkness that surrounded that question. Is it not enough to make billions from other kinds of investments, even off the naiveté of others? Or is it a great hoax? What about the explosion that destroyed the foyer of Richard Melmont's mansion? What was that all about? Could Melmont have been responsible for the explosion himself in order to dramatize the significance of the project, to plant the suspicion that unknown dark forces were interested? The immediate family of Richard Melmont felt themselves in thrall of some kind of inexplicable wickedness and they had to extricate themselves. Maria Melmont would not seek a divorce. But she would no longer preside at Richard Melmont's lunches and soirees and balls. Barbara and Daniel, who owed their father much, had also lost much in having a father almost in name only. They had to extricate themselves from this tangled web. Jacob's decision to cut himself off from his father-in-law was easiest of all. Their common history did not go back to birth and childhood. No deep emotions, however turbulent, existed. He was unabashedly repelled by Richard Melmont's exclusive service to self, his indifference to the predicament of others, his hardness. Even more so as Jacob dreamed dreams of a possible world, as he thought, were the possibility of this possible world widely known. But men like Richard Melmont had the means to establish what the facts were, and they excluded the possibilities dreamed of by all the idealistic Jacobs and Jills of this world.

We shall have to arrange a meeting with your father. Jacob, you should not be present. Only Barbara, Daniel, and I should be present. The issues between us are too fraught with heartache for you to be included in such a meeting.

The meeting day arrived. Maria Melmont spoke. We think that you are embarked on a course that could end tragically. We implore you to stop. We know that you will not. We will cut off contact with you. With great regret. Should you stop what we think can end tragically we will come back to you. I will not seek a divorce. I will be your nominal wife. I have no desire to embarrass you. But I will no longer preside at your social affairs.

The resulting explosion, denunciation, bellowing, and gesticulating were menacing and horrific. No divorce? I will divorce. No end to family? I will end family. No end of money flowing from my pocket to yours? I will end money flowing from my pocket to yours. No thought of being paupers? You will be paupers. No thought of my position in the world? I will take care of my position in the world. No love? No affection? No respect? I will find love, affection, and respect on my own terms. Such was the gist of Richard Melmont's tirade, after which he strode out of the parlor, shut the front door not quietly, entered his limousine, and was driven off.

Maria, Barbara, Daniel, shaken, of course. But not surprised. Maria Melmont would sell her modest mansion and move into a more modest apartment. As a writer of novels and essays she would survive. And not too badly by the ways of the world. Barbara Melmont and her spouse Jacob Rosen would also move to a more modest apartment. As lawyers they too would survive. And not too badly by the ways of the world. Daniel Melmont would move in with his mother for the present. As an economist he would have to find ways to make money. But he too would survive. And by the ways of the world not too badly.

The reader needs to know that the expected happened a few days after the stormy meeting. Barbara gave birth to a girl and the parents named her Clara.

Chapter Twenty-One

Exposure of a Hoax

The share price of Dark Energy Systems had risen substantially above the price at the time of the initial public offering. Richard Melmont decided that the time had come to sell his shares. He did sell his shares and made a substantial profit, quite substantial. He whispered in the ear of a friend on the Senate Armed Services Committee that he had sold his shares. His friend whispered in the ear of a friend of his in the Senate a similar message. He or she—the author cannot be sure who—let it be known to a friend in the House that the time had come to sell shares in Dark Energy Systems and he or she casually mentioned the same to a friend in the administration and through a series of whispers the information spread into the ears of other members of the administration and then leaked out into the ears of the CEOs of the largest banks and hedge funds. All these shares were bought up by investors whose ears had not gotten whispered into.

Meanwhile George Banat developed a terrible backache. He knew something about dark energy and recognized a fraud when he saw it. He spoke to the senator who had held his peace at the closed-door hearing. The senator who held his peace had his own misgivings and took the trouble of consulting an astrophysicist who was abreast of developments concerning dark energy and related matters such as Higgs bosons, neutrinos, quarks, and hadrons, concerning which the reader is surely familiar. Research was ongoing, of course, but we, meaning the astrophysicists, were not sure of the way all these particles fit together or even if they all existed outside the imaginations of the pioneers who imagined them. Dark energy, a powerful concept that knit all space together, if it, dark energy, existed as presently conceived. But dark energy as a force that could be captured and put to use as one might put to use the atom in atomic energy, a fantasy suitable for science fiction. The senator who held his peace is a very careful senator and he consulted several other astrophysicists and was treated to the same revelations.

The senator who had held his peace spoke to the chairman of the Senate Armed Services Committee and suggested that the committee hold an open hearing and invite the previously mentioned eminent astrophysicists to testify. Such a hearing had a certain compelling appeal to it and an open hearing was duly scheduled, this time with a full complement of newspaper, TV, and Internet pundits in attendance. Before the hearing was adjourned, the share price of Dark Energy Systems had plummeted to near zero. Investors who had not had their ears whispered into were up in arms. Non-investors were up in arms. The pundits were up in arms. The administration, Senate, and House were up in arms, even those whose ears had been whispered into and had made substantial profits on their shares in Dark Energy Systems before they had plummeted in value to near zero, were up in arms.

Public wrath turned toward Richard Melmont, but he steadfastly maintained that the research institutes affiliated with Dark Energy Systems were on the right track and great results would have emerged had they been given more time. But since funds had run out, time had run out. Moreover, China, Russia, or Germany might now steal a march on us. No one knew what the researchers for Dark Energy Systems thought because they had been required to sign confidentiality agreements and were to regard their work as top-secret military research. But a rumor got around that several of the researchers had privately come to the senator who had held his peace and compelled him to hold his peace no longer. George Banat became the most popular figure on the TV talk shows as the most persuasive debunker of Melmont's pseudo-science and in a matter of days had published a book on the subject.

Richard Melmont stood in defiance against all the agitation in his conviction that the world works like this because the world works like this, always has and always will, and it cannot work the way it cannot work.

Was this a hoax perpetrated by Richard Melmont or was he its victim save for the billions that he made? The author is unable to penetrate such secrets, for the difference between the will to believe and the perpetration of a hoax is sometimes impenetrable to all but the one believing or perpetrating. This is one of those times. In any case, it is not a violation of the law to be wrong, certainly not a crime.

Chapter Twenty-Two

Richard Melmont on the Beach

Richard Melmont spoke to his estate manager, John Stevens. I would like to walk along the beach. I would like you to walk with me. The request was unprecedented. Melmont did not socialize with his household employees.

As you say, sir. I will certainly come along with you.

It's a fine day, John. Sun streaming, cloudless sky, water calm.

Yes, sir. So it is.

I have been wronged, John. My family has wronged me. My wife, my daughter, my son. They have wronged me. They have gone against me. Don't you think I was wronged, John?

It is not my place to have opinions about family matters. It is my place to manage your estate and do as you wish. That has been my policy for twenty-five years.

But I ask you man to man, have I not been wronged?

If you insist on having my opinion, you have been wronged. (What else could he say?)

So I thought. So I know. Come what may, a family is a family.

Yes, a family is a family, come what may. (No contradicting the facts.)

The world is against me, too. But I don't care for the opinions of the world. (And yet he does.)

The world doesn't care for me and I don't care for the world. So we're even.

So you say. You are even. (Perhaps not.)

Have I done evil? No, I have not. I have helped myself. Everyone helps himself. Don't you? That is not evil. I am bitter, bitter. My family has made me bitter. The world has made me bitter. I have done all in my power to give to my family. I have given to the world what I could. Should I walk into the sea and not turn back? Just keep walking?

Certainly not. Certainly not.

I wouldn't. I wouldn't think of it. I am strong. I have done all that I have done by myself, by my wits. Why should I now question myself, question what I have done, question what I have accomplished, question what I have earned by my own efforts? I shall not question myself.

No, you will not.

Could I be mistaken? Have I done wrong somehow? Do others see what I don't see? No. Certainly not. The world is a hard place, John. You must be hard in a hard place. Others see that, don't they? To think otherwise is pretense. Leave that to others. Let them pretend, not knowing that they pretend. Who ever turns the other cheek? Fine for ministers to say who pretend to live in another world. Fine for mediocre men to say, who don't even know what world they are living in. Let them rise up and be hard. Let them be hard for their own benefit. What a joke. The weak men don't even know it is a joke.

I am alone, John. I am alone with billions. And I mean to do with them as I choose. Give some to causes? Why not? Make a way for myself? Why not? Help men loyal to me? Why not?

They walked in silence, Melmont continuing to justify his ways to himself, Stevens thinking Melmont had lost everything of value in life, yet raved on, trapped in his own delusions.

A woman walked on the beach toward them. The woman was Maria Melmont. Richard Melmont hurried forward. She turned and walked away.

The Rise and Fall of President Barry Blue

Contents

Chapter One

Who Is This Man?

I asked myself, who is Barry Blue? When I asked myself that question about Bill Clinton, I wrote *Through a Crooked Mirror*. Then I asked the same question about George W. Bush and wrote *The Family Business*. I think that I came up with satisfactory answers. At any rate, they satisfied me. I can say with all modesty that they satisfied the reviewers too.

Here is the procedure for gaining access to the West Wing. I ask the press secretary if I might interview members of the administration from the president on down. After two weeks in the present case, the answer came. Yes, I could do the interviews provided that "off the record" truly meant off the record. Given the popularity of my previous books, no surprise there. I was thinking, get inside the machinery of the Blue administration and see how it works. Then I can answer the question: Who is Barry Blue?

On my first visit, I passed the president in the hallway.

"What malicious gossip are you going to write about me?"

"Not a word, sir."

Chapter Two

The Orphan

Veronica Starrett is President Blue's most trusted advisor after his wife Madeleine. She also knows more about the young Barry Blue than anyone else I can think of. Since I wanted to begin at the beginning, I made an appointment with Starrett. When the time came for the interview, we sat down at opposite ends of a sofa in her office, with me scribbling away as she talked.

I opened the conversation on a positive note. "I think I know something about the president's childhood. Let's skip the part about where he was born. The fabrications are absurd."

"Right. He was born in Hawaii. From the beginning he felt like an orphan. He saw his father once for a fleeting moment. Then Barry Blue Senior went back to Kenya, got mixed up in politics on the losing side, got drunk, and killed himself in a car accident. By the way, you might think Barry Blue is an unusual name for a black Kenyan. Don't forget that English was the masters' language.

"Well, his mother left him to do her anthropological thing in Indonesia. So she dumped him too, but at least on her parents in Hawaii. They taught him that he was both white and black. That was confusing. How could he be both? He didn't know who he was. Here's a teenager trying to figure it out. He thought he chose black. He didn't choose. His skin chose. After that, he pretended to be outgoing. He wasn't."

I asked, "Is it true that you spied a brilliant young man and took him under your wing?"

"Yes. His future wife Madeleine worked under me as an attorney in the mayor's office in Chicago. When she met him, she saw that he was brilliant. So brilliant that routine work bored him. I introduced him to the establishment in Chicago. Everybody wanted to be Barry's mentor. Lawyering bored him. Organizing bored him. The state legislature bored him. Congress bored him. Yah, yah, yah, as he said. Against impossible odds, he got himself nominated, and that against the most well-oiled political machine imaginable. And he beat the machine with his eloquence."

"What about the presidency," I asked. "Does it bore him?"

"No. He finally found something that doesn't bore him."

"He has a reputation for being aloof," I said.

"What do you expect from a man with his childhood?"

"Then who is Barry Blue? He campaigned on 'Change You Can Believe In,' but change has been compromised to death."

"Look. His father was a radical. He lined up with the wrong side. His enemies destroyed him. Barry will not line up with the wrong side. Barry will not go the way of his father. Barry will line up with power. He not only has to redeem his father, but also his mother, his grandparents, and when it comes to that, the whole country."

"Then who is this man who says one thing to get elected and does another after he wins?"

Veronica Starrett looked at me with a smile. "He is just who I said he is."

Chapter Three

John Falstaff

Veronica Starrett advised me to interview John Falstaff first. No, not that one. The one who was President Blue's high school English teacher. John Falstaff could tell me who Blue really was. He and Blue had formed a close friendship. Blue had invited Falstaff to the White House as an informal advisor. He could tell Blue how things really were, not how his advisors saw things through the distorted lens of self-interest. I asked to talk with Falstaff, but the conversations were to be off the record. I took notes for myself alone.

I met Falstaff in his West Wing office early one afternoon toward the beginning of President Blue's second term. Falstaff remarkably resembles his fictional predecessor: short, rotund, ruddy in the face, sporting a scraggly white beard.

After a few amenities, I got straight to my subject: Who is Barry Blue?

"I've known President Blue for thirty-five years. I have to admit that after all this time I still have no idea who he is. I know what he says and I know what he does. They don't match up. Don't forget. What I tell you is off the record. I wouldn't repeat anything like this in public."

"Believe me, I'm not going to write who said what without permission. The question is, what makes you think that he says one thing and does another?"

"I've had frank conversations with the president over the past several years. That's why he asked me to come here.

To have frank conversations. To hold up a mirror to him so he can see himself. I'm giving you the impressions I've taken away from those conversations."

"For example?"

"All right. Let's start at the beginning when he won the 2008 election, when he gave a victory speech to a hundred-thousand supporters who were mad for him, they thought he was the new messiah. You remember phrases like America is a place where all things are possible, this is your victory, we will get there, we will reclaim the American dream, yes we can?

"Well, what did he do? He saved Wall Street. But did he do anything great for anybody else? In a rich country where the public is worse off than the public of all the other rich countries?"

"So what does the president say to that?"

"He says that he has to deal with the world as it is. The rich have power. He has to deal with it."

"But," I said, "he had the public behind him after the election. He had the power. He let it slip away. What does he say to that?"

"He says movements are transient. The public is amorphous. The public slips away when it doesn't get what it wants when it wants it. The rich are here to stay. They call the tune. They say the country will straighten itself out by itself, but we have to straighten out the world. So he sends more troops to Afghanistan because they say so. He asked me to go to Afghanistan and tell him the true story.

"I replied: What if I am wounded? What if I am killed? It would be honorable to go, no doubt. Can honor set a leg? No. Or an arm? No. Or take away the grief of a wound? No. Honor has no skill in surgery, then? No. What is honor? A word. What is in that word 'honor'? Air. A trim reckoning.

Who has it? He that died on Wednesday. Does he feel it? No. Does he hear it? No. It is insensible then? Yes, to the dead. But will it not live with the living? No. Why? Detraction will not suffer it. Therefore, I will have none of it. Honor is a mere escutcheon.

"The president jumped up from his desk and shouted at me, 'Get out of here! I can't take any more of this.'"

Chapter Four

An Unexpected Guest

Almost a week later, I spoke with John Falstaff again. He was agitated. "What I have to say is off the record. So far off the record that you can't even take notes. Not a word of this can be repeated to anyone."

That certainly got my attention. I began to wonder if I could write a book on the Barry Blue presidency directly from my own observations or would have to resort to secondary sources. Here's what I remember about the conversation.

The president was in the Oval Office between meetings chatting with Madeleine about summer plans for their two teenage sons, Manny and Sam. His assistant called on the intercom to say that a George Washington had passed through security and was standing at her desk and was sure that President Blue would be interested in talking with him. "He looks like, to be frank, like George Washington."

The president asked Madeleine's advice and she said, "Sounds like some kind of actor. Maybe he has Hollywood connections. Chat with him for a few minutes. What do you have to lose?"

The president called back on the intercom. "All right. Send him in." In walked a reasonable facsimile of George Washington.

"Thank you for taking the time to see me, President Blue," he said as President Blue asked his visitor to take a seat.

"I cannot believe what has happened in these United States during the last 237 years since we signed the Declaration of Independence. I drove over to the White House in an auto-MObile. I'm puzzled why I wasn't driven over in a carriage drawn by horses."

"The word is pronounced AUTO-mobile, Mr. Washington," Blue replied.

"I love the smell of horses. I love the look of horses. You have taken a step backward with the AUTO-mobile, as you say. And by the way, no umbrage taken, but I am used to being called President Washington."

"Beg pardon, President Washington. On the matter of horses, we still do have horses around, and I will be pleased to arrange for you to ride a thoroughbred."

"I am gratified to you for that offer. Before I forget, I want to say that I am honored that you named this former swamp Washington. I am honored that you have erected a monument dedicated to me. But why did it have to be a phallic symbol?"

"Beg pardon, President Washington. We don't think of it that way."

"Another thing that bothers me is this constant touching and blabbing into a little box. Don't people want to speak to each other anymore?"

Here Madeleine spoke up. "The little boxes are useful. You can talk with people far away and learn a great deal by touching the right spots on what we call the screen. But frankly, Mr. President, the inattention to the world around us bothers me too. How can you ever look at the color of the sky or children playing or taste your food if you're constantly preoccupied with the little box?"

At this point, the Blues looked at each other surreptitiously with incredulous expressions that said, "Can this be the real George Washington?"

"Well, President Washington," said Barry Blue, wanting to have a serious conversation. "Aren't you proud of the country that you launched as the pre-eminent founder?"

"No, I am not. In hindsight I regret that we went to war with the British. That was rash. We should have been patient and discussed our differences with them. Look at Canada. They gradually freed themselves from British tutelage without war. They gained by staying in an empire that helped them mediate their differences. They treated their native peoples better than we did. They became a more civilized country than we did."

"But," said Blue, "we had the intractable problem of slavery."

"The presence of British power might well have prevented a civil war. We made a terrible mistake in forming one country instead of two. The absurdity of counting slaves as three-fifths of a person has no equal. I accept my responsibility for error.

"You are insufferably rigid in regarding a Constitution written in 1789 as applicable for all time. The presidency, the Senate, the House, the Supreme Court are pawns moved around by the highest bidder. We should have inserted a clause requiring the Constitution to be rewritten every 25 years. I suppose a rewritten Constitution would go to the highest bidder too. But at least the public might have an opportunity to ask, what's best for us now?"

"You, President Washington, also had to deal with entrenched interests."

"Yes, we had Jefferson on the side of the landlords and Hamilton on the side of the bankers. We had free states and we had slave states. We acted blindly. Now you have the rich and the poor. Haven't you learned anything?"

"I am doing my best."

"It isn't good enough. These United States are at war with one another."

"I have another appointment, Mr. President. Thank you for dropping by. I will arrange for you to meet some thoroughly civilized horses."

"Thank you for your time. I never expected to see a black president."

Chapter Five

Another Unexpected Guest

I'm dubious about this, but a few days later I was sitting in the White House cafeteria having a snack with the president's receptionist, Willow, and an intern named Michael, her fiancé. She tells me that the president and Secretary of State Jon Ferry entered the Oval Office at 9 a.m. last Monday and found a tall, slender, bearded man walking around looking at the pictures and memorabilia. "The president told me," she said, "that he must have forgotten an appointment. He said, 'welcome.' I have to make it clear that this story is definitely off the record. Only Michael and I know about it except for the president and secretary of state. Probably the first lady too."

Here we go again, I thought. Will I ever hear about anything that's on the record?

The tall, slender, bearded man said, "I just had to sleep in the Lincoln Bedroom last night. It was my office when I was president. My successors did well with the furnishings. They're mid-nineteenth century, which made me feel right at home."

Barry Blue perked up. "President?"

"Oh, beg pardon. I forgot to introduce myself. I'm President Abraham Lincoln. I decided to come back and see what's happened since the horrible Civil War. Please forgive me for walking into the Oval Office, as you call it. In my time there was no Oval Office. Just my rectangular room."

The president and secretary of state looked at each other incredulously. But they had heard of marvelous feats performed through nanotechnology, including the reconstruction of human organs. Maybe news hadn't reached them about reconstructing entire human beings.

"You certainly look like Lincoln," the president said.

"Yes. I know what you mean. As I once remarked, 'If I were two-faced, would I be wearing this one?'"

The president waved away the remark and said, "We like your face. We have put it on all our pennies."

"Yes. I hear that pennies are nearly worthless. In my time, pennies were worth something. When I was a clerk, I walked three miles to return six pennies to a woman. She forgot to pick them up off the counter."

"Your picture also appears on five-dollar bills."

"And Grover Cleveland's picture appears on thousand-dollar bills."

"We have an imposing statue of you seated at the Lincoln Memorial on the National Mall."

"I don't believe in graven images. Worthless pennies are a more fitting memorial for me."

"How can you say that? You saved the Union and rank with George Washington, who started it."

"I can never forgive myself for blundering into a civil war. I did not anticipate that 400,000 men would be killed. Millions of family members and friends grieved. These are wounds that cannot be bound up. As many men, women, and children died or grieved for those who died as there were slaves. Four million slaves. Four million dead or grieving. Can you measure one against the other?"

"I can't answer a moral question with a mathematical equation. Slavery was an unmitigated evil."

"So it was. But I perpetrated another unmitigated evil. The North won the war but the South won the peace. Instead of uniting the nation, I broke it into two parts. Instead of freeing the slaves, I perpetrated semi-slavery.

"If I had better judgment, I would have acted more wisely. Suppose I had taken the huge sums that paid for the war and used them to buy the manumission of slaves? Suppose I had appealed to abolitionists to compensate recalcitrant slave owners for any loss they might sustain from freeing their slaves? Suppose I had transferred public lands to freed slaves? Better to buy peace than to make an enemy.

"If I had taken these actions, the United States would have remained the United States instead of the dis-United States. It remains the dis-United States to this day. The enmity of the Civil War still hangs over us. It poisons all civil discourse. The Civil War is not over. I am to blame! I am damnably to blame!"

"We only know in hindsight," the secretary of state said in words of consolation.

"If only Reconstruction had not been unreconstructed," President Blue mused.

Lincoln stroked his beard. "That would have required deporting all the slaveholders to Africa."

"You are right. You cannot make history that refuses to be made."

"Do not use that as an excuse for yourself, Mr. President."

Then the grave Lincoln walked away.

Chapter Six

The New Deal Reprised

A few weeks later, more or less, President Blue and his national security advisor, Su-Ann Ross, enter the Oval Office to review the withdrawal from Afghanistan. Franklin Roosevelt and his secretary of labor, Frances Perkins, are engaged in an animated conversation. They greet President Blue and Su-Ann Ross courteously. "Thank you for allowing us to meet you. I'm beginning to believe in time travel."

"So am I," replied President Blue.

"I hardly recognize the country. The last I remember, we were winning World War II."

"You did a great job in leading the Allies to victory."

"Perhaps I did. But looking back, I see that I committed terrible crimes."

"You can't be serious."

"I am quite serious. I allowed our air force to fire bomb and kill innocent, men, women, and children. I didn't restrain the British from doing the same. What good did it do to destroy Dresden instead of the nearby railroads and munitions plants?"

"War makes us mad. You surely thought that bombing Dresden would shorten the war."

"It lengthened the war. It made the Germans dig in. I should have bombed the railways to the concentration camps. I was guilty of anti-Semitism. My State Department was guilty of anti-Semitism. I have had plenty of time to think it over. I see the public attitude has changed."

"Well, you were a man of your times. We all are."

"What sense did it make to round up all the Japanese in California and put them in camps? They were loyal Americans. Of course we didn't do that to German-Americans. They weren't Asians."

"You've got a point there," replied Su-Ann Ross. "You also allowed the military to give the dirtiest, meanest work to blacks. We've come a long way since the 1940s." Ms. Ross happens to be black.

"I was guilty of racial prejudice. I've had time to think it over."

"But let's look at the balance sheet. You won the war." So said President Blue, in a thoughtful mood.

"We can look at the balance sheet. Still, on the cost side I made the mistake of choosing that idiot Harry Truman to run with me as Vice President in 1944. A sane man would never have dropped atom bombs on Hiroshima and Nagasaki when we knew that Japan was within days of surrendering."

"We really didn't know that, Mr. President. Our most important mission was to save the lives of American servicemen," replied President Blue.

"If that were the case, why didn't we drop the bomb on an uninhabited Japanese island so they could see what we could do?"

"We can't re-run history."

"When you come back after 68 years, you do re-run history through your mind."

"I insist, Sir, that the main things are that you won the war and saved the economy from the Great Depression."

"Yes, Einstein told me about the bombs and told me that we had to get the jump on the Nazis in developing them. And Keynes told me about deficit finance to get us out of the depression. But I didn't understand Keynes and acted out of necessity to rescue the unemployed, thanks to the insistence of Frances Perkins."

"We didn't understand the economics of it," said Frances Perkins. "In 1936 we stopped spending and the Depression began all over again. When World War II approached, we had no choice but to go head-over-heels into debt to build a war machine. And that ended the Depression."

"Mr. President," said Roosevelt, "you now understand Keynesian economics and yet you haven't ended your depression. You have millions out of work. You have millions who have been thrown out of their homes. You rescued the bankers instead of the unemployed. With all due respect, what is the problem?"

"You know how limited the power of the president is. I'm trying, but I have powerful forces that I have to placate."

"Let me be blunt. That's malarkey. I went against the establishment. I told them to go to hell. I was backed by the public. The public and I pushed back against the establishment and they didn't recover until a president came along that put them back in power. Thank you Ronald Reagan."

"I'm working to turn things around."

"No you're not, President Blue. You have carried on where George W. Bush left off."

"The times were different. You had powerful unions behind you."

Frances Perkins replied, "President Roosevelt helped build the powerful unions. What have you done?"

"The time for unions has passed, Madam Secretary. Robots are replacing people."

"But the rich are benefiting instead of the public. Why can't the public benefit from robots too, have more and work less?"

"My national security advisor Su-Ann Ross and I have some pressing matters to deal with, Mr. President and Madam Secretary. The Middle East, you know. My wife and sons would be delighted to meet you if you would be so kind as to drop in on them."

Chapter Seven

More of the Same!

I'm just repeating what I've been told by John Falstaff. Is he making all this up? He swears that Blue was mystified and shaken when he related these encounters. And he had witnesses with him. And it's all off the record. I can't tell you how frustrated I am. Something paranormal is going on or the president is insane. I'll probably write this up and publish it sometime in the future. Maybe as fiction. I just don't know.

But you haven't heard the end. The next Wednesday morning at 9 a.m. President Blue walked into the Oval Office in a state of apprehension. He could not accept the idea of meeting unexpected guests. Guests from the past. He did not believe in reincarnation. What kind of phenomenon was he experiencing, he wondered? He had had a staff member with him each time. They had experienced the same—hallucinations? Extrasensory perceptions? Tricks? What?

Oh my God! Lyndon Johnson is sitting in the wing chair reading *From Lyndon Johnson to Barry Blue* by Rob Woodruff!

"Pardon the intrusion," said Johnson. "I am allowed a furlough from hell one day a year for my good deeds. This year I thought I'd come and have a conversation with my astute successor, Barry Blue.

"I think my good deeds are well known. The Civil Rights Act. The Voting Rights Act. Medicare. Medicaid. The War on Poverty. You know, every good deed that added up to The Great Society. I knew that my actions would cost the Demo-

crats the South. I never imagined that the South would rein-
carnate the Confederacy.

"You know, I got to be president by chance, as we all do.
The vice presidency wasn't worth a bucket of warm piss, as
my predecessor John Nance Garner said. What a horrible way
to become president. I awake at night in terror."

Accepting the inevitability of a conversation, Barry Blue
responded. "I admire what you accomplished. I wouldn't be
president were it not for your accomplishments. The South
will eventually rejoin the Union. The young will have it that
way. The days of the New Confederacy are numbered."

"Let me ask you a blunt question," replied Lyndon Johnson. "You had a movement behind you when you were elected president in 2008. You could have pushed on things that
I started. But you didn't lead. You allowed the movement to
fade away."

"I am dealing with a complex situation that forces me to
compromise."

"My situation was complicated too. But I stood eye to eye
with congressmen and told them that I would get their bill
passed, I would raise money for them, I would get them re-
elected. But for Christ's sake, you've got to help me now. And
if you don't, I will leak information about your affair with
that pretty little intern on your staff. And by God, I got their
support. I used the 'Johnson treatment,' as it was called. Why
don't you try it?

"You might end up with compromise. But you don't start
with compromise. You say one thing and do another. I don't
know who you are, Mr. President."

"It's too early to judge. I'm doing good works. I face an
opposition that won't compromise. And the most complicated world . . . "

"Complicated world! If I knew then what I know now, I would never have mired us down in Vietnam. I thought the whole Far East would fall to communism if it wasn't stopped in Vietnam. I will forever be horrified by the killing I caused—for nothing.

"You have blood on your hands the way I did. Surge in Afghanistan? You ought to know that Afghanistan is a hopeless cause. I don't understand who you are.

"My time is up. Back to hell with all the other presidents of the United States. At least we have good conversations. See you soon."

Chapter Eight

This Can't Go On!

"Good to see you," said President Barry Blue, as he entered his office at eight in the morning, resigned to seemingly endless encounters with presidents from the past.

"I thought I'd drop by and see how things are going," replied Ronald Reagan. "The first thing I see is that it's not Morning in America."

"We have problems, but we're solving them," replied Barry Blue.

"Doesn't appear that way to me. When I look back a quarter of a century, I see that it wasn't Morning in America then either. It was twilight. Someone coined the word 'Reaganomics'—supply-side economics. Reduce taxes to spur growth, control the money supply to reduce inflation, reduce government spending, deregulate the economy, take a hard line against unions. I now see how wrong I was. I was even talking about welfare queens driving Cadillacs. I don't remember who made up that line for me."

"You're very bold to admit that you were wrong."

"Why don't you do the same, Barry? You told the public 'Yes We Can,' but you govern as a president who says 'Yes We Can' to the banks. Who are you, Barry Blue? I was wrong, but at least I was consistent."

"Don't forget what kind of Congress I'm dealing with," replied President Blue. "I'm working for the public, but they're trying to block every move I make."

"You're definitely not the 'Teflon president,' as I was called. My sunny manner allowed me to sidestep all the blame for mistakes. I approved the Iran-Contra affair in 1986 but I didn't get the blame. I claimed ignorance."

"We are trying to track down terrorists by monitoring everybody's email, and I get the blame instead of credit for foiling terrorist attacks."

"Try being sunny and don't appear so defensive. A display of sunniness will work miracles for you."

"I try to be sunny. Haven't you seen me smile in public?"

"But you have to lead while you're smiling. Nobody's going to smile back when you send Americans to get killed in Afghanistan and you have nothing to show for it. I called Russia 'the evil empire.' I at least convinced Gorbachev to reduce our nuclear arsenals. Then he got too far ahead of the political establishment and they threw him out. They gave that fool Yeltsin a chance to wreck the country. But I'm starting to talk like Machiavelli."

President Blue began thinking about Putin. I'll be completely gray by the time my second term ends. Then maybe Harriet Clifton will take over . . .

Blue snapped back to attention. "Machiavelli. Pros and cons about him."

"Well, never mind Machiavelli. Think of Washington, Lincoln, Roosevelt, Johnson. I've got to go now."

"Oh my God," said President Blue to no one in particular, as Ronald Reagan walked away.

That afternoon President Blue left for Afghanistan to meet with the leading clique in Kabul. The following evening he went into the surrounding hills and found himself standing in a vast sea of dead American soldiers saluting him. Shortly afterwards he stood in a vast sea of dead Afghani men, women, and children in various stages of decomposition.

Chapter Nine

The Secretary and the Intern

You remember Willow and Michael, right? Well, soon after President Blue returned from his trip to Afghanistan, I had lunch with them in the West Wing cafeteria. They didn't look too happy. They got into an argument that, frankly, embarrassed me.

Willow: "I defend the president. What about health care for millions? He's doing everything he can under the circumstances."

Michael: "I can't work for him anymore. He betrayed everything he stood for. Or said he stood for. He left a vacuum for the Tea Party to fill. He can't even control his own departments. He can't even close Guantánamo. Sure, he did a few good things. But, my God! Drones? Kill innocent families? And then say, 'I'm really good at killing people.' I QUIT!"

At this point I excused myself and left the table. I didn't want to be in the middle of a brawl between two lovers. A tittle-tattle at an adjoining table told me what I missed. Michael called Blue a Don Quixote: he lives in an imaginary world. Or does he? Then Michael threw this one out. Blue was a better man when he followed Jeremiah Wright. Yes, Wright said God *damn* America for all its hypocrisies and self-righteous blabber. Sure, that's intemperate speech. But at least you can't accuse him of hypocrisy.

Willow: "Don Quixote? Jeremiah Wright? You are delusional!"

Michael: "You are delusional!"

Willow: "You realize our engagement is off!"

Michael: "I'll say it's off. Off! Off! Off!"

Everyone in the cafeteria stared as the decibels increased. What can I say? That was the end of what appeared to be a beautiful romance.

Blue and Falstaff

Falstaff: "I've told you the way it is."

Blue: "You don't understand what I'm trying to do and what I'm up against. I want you to leave the White House."

Falstaff: "You can't stand to hear the truth. Your rise and fall was swift."

Blue: "Get out."

Persona Non Grata

You remember my first interview with Veronica Starrett, President Blue's mentor and most trusted advisor, after his wife Madeleine, of course. She gave me permission to interview White House staff members as well as the president himself, provided that I wouldn't publish anything that was off the record. This, my last interview, was a sad ending to what seemed to be a golden opportunity to write an insider's view of what was going on in the Blue White House.

"I know that you relied heavily on John Falstaff to learn what's been going on in the White House," she said. "Unfortunately, he proved to be a false friend. He made up hostile stories about the president. Or he was delusional. We're here to protect the president, not vilify him. In any case, Falstaff is gone. Everything you learned, and I mean everything, is officially off the record and, I'm sorry, an interview with the president is out of the question. Why didn't you interview friends of the president? I'm afraid that I'll have to revoke your White House press credentials effective immediately. We know what we know because we monitored your conversations."

I made an appeal about my objectivity. I did interview friends of the president and intended to interview more of them. Starrett herself told me to interview Falstaff. Told me he was a close friend of the president. I feel bad about being thrown out and more so about being regarded as unreliable. I can't assess Falstaff's reliability. Maybe he was telling the truth and maybe he wasn't. I'm going to write my book about President Blue anyway. I assure you that it will all be taken from secondary sources. But my sense of what was going on in the White House is not off the record. I already have a title for my book. I will call it *The Rise and Fall of President Barry Blue.*